SANKOFA

A Southern Tale

J.K. Pascall

authorHOUSE®

AuthorHouse™
1663 Liberty Drive
Bloomington, IN 47403
www.authorhouse.com
Phone: 1 (800) 839-8640

Published by AuthorHouse 04/02/2019

ISBN: 978-1-7283-0679-7 (sc)
ISBN: 978-1-7283-0677-3 (hc)
ISBN: 978-1-7283-0678-0 (e)

Library of Congress Control Number: 2019903923

Contents

CHAPTER ONE

Arrival

Taurus born, Thomas Celestine came into the world kicking and screaming. He was of mixed heritage. His great grandmother arrived on a boat from India. His father's very dark, smooth skin and jet black wavy hair reflected his Caribbean origin. His mother's family arrived in Trinidad before 1900 and his father's settled there in the early 1930s. Four bloodlines collide on 8th May, 1954 to introduce possibility, probability and hope for a future better than theirs. In a time when nationhood was being nurtured in the Caribbean region and Trinidad was dealing with the dichotomy of politics vs intellectualism, there was hope. Thomas's family lived in San Fernando, a town on the south western coast of the island, a hub of sorts for agricultural products and textiles, but mostly the home of industry. The major races mixed heavily in this area and bred a culture slightly removed from the traditional rigid polarised origins.

Thomas's mother was a simple woman, religious and pious, with a pleasant demeanour. She grew up as a 'tom boy' always trying to measure up to her big brothers. She lifted weights and tried to stay close to her big brothers by engaging in the same pursuits as them like weight lifting but traditional roles dictated that she be kept on a shorter leash than her brothers. She adored her mother though and was obedient. Beryl was elated to give her husband a son at twenty three. They had not been married long, so Thomas was a sign that all was right with the world. Karl was happy to be married to a woman that he loved for some time prior to their courtship. He was seven years her senior, but he admired her spirit, her innocence and her frankness. He would tease her in passing by telling her that one day she would be his wife. He was a man of few words, drawn within himself as though he was still reeling from the trauma of some long-gone childhood drama. He only came out of that shell for his three loves, football, bodybuilding and Beryl. He was a little man who sculpted a beautiful physique. She would taunt him about his chicken chest and little bird wings. She knew she won a prize man, and considered herself fortunate though he had other lovers, Beryl was his love to end all searching.

Ma, as everyone called her, was born in 1898 just before the turn of the century. She was quiet, resilient and mysterious. Mother to five children, two boys and three girls, she was known for her sewing and baking skills. She always kept Beryl close and her grandchild Thomas, was a favourite. There was something mystical about Ma and pleasant radiance seemed to emanate from her. Some said that she had the gift of sight. Beryl always took her warnings seriously. Despite the negative things people said about him, Ma approved of her daughter's union. They settled into a simple, happy existence. Karl pursued his hobbies while supporting his family and Beryl took care of Thomas at home.

Beryl's big brothers had a strange hobby of their own, they were passionate about 'Black Indian mas' and would dress up in costumes at Carnival time and paint their skins with various dyes and portray the Native American. Beryl did not share this interest but her husband did. He was well-known in the San Fernando street parade as the short black man with his face painted black and white, carrying a round shield on his right arm and short axe in his left. They brought life to this mas for years with feathers, tassels smocks, the works. They entertained some, frightened some and competed with other bands during the festival. San Fernando was teaming with mas: drunken sailor mas, jab jab mas, robber mas, devil mas and Black and Red Indian mas. Thomas's uncles were developing their art while learning to speak a local version of the Red Indian language and mimicking their tribal movements. This all culminated in a street display where one Indian band leader would block the other in the street and have a verbal contest while the public judged them on appearance, movement and speech. It was not a guaranteed spectacle. There were only a few men trained in the art of duelling.

Carnival 1956 saw one such duel in which a band of Black Indians from Broadway in San Fernando were stopped by a band from Coffee Street, and an epic duel played out much to the delight of the spectators. The leader from Broadway was declared the winner and the Red Indians had to clear the way for Black to pass and for the most part they did. The tail enders of the band however broke out into a skirmish and the two bands were drawn into a bloody exchange with axes and cutlasses and knives. Three men fell that day, while many more were wounded. Thomas's uncles brought Karl's limp body home to Beryl. They laid him out in full costume at her feet. The noise from the yard was unbearable. He was a favourite and would be missed forever. How could this happen? This was the worst clash ever. People mourned that everyone loved him and couldn't imagine who would kill him?

In San Fernando, 1956 carried a kind of heaviness, a tense expectation that had folks on edge. Could this have crept into the mas and caused this ridiculous outcome? Beryl did not care. She wailed until she lost her voice and did not speak for two years. No one could pinpoint the exact day she regained her voice. And what of Thomas? Oblivious to the political climate and the events of Carnival, all he knew was that his daddy would not be coming home again. The new reality that he had no father would stay with him forever. Two years old and without his daddy, Thomas's loss created a ripple effect that would be felt by many. Ma was a rock. Her presence and unwavering support buffered Beryl. She gave Beryl more than enough time to grieve. Her example of calm needed more than ever. She would say, 'Beryl don't worry child, everything will be ok'. Beryl would not answer but they knew, it was their own strange language that they had developed over the years. The lesson translated to enduring your hardship with grace. They never asked why, they just did, and knew that it was better that way.

Her mute years allowed Beryl to contemplate why Karl's mother blamed her for his death, why she had to lose her husband and if she was being punished for getting married in the first place. Since she was a child, she had thoughts of becoming a nun but she loved Karl and now he had been taken away. Beryl had not been educated beyond primary school and she tried to understand her life within her limited learning and experience. She had Thomas to take care of and was motivated to persevere regardless. Taking care of Thomas was a priority which motivated her.

Meanwhile on the national scene the People's National Movement (PNM) was the elected party in Government and there was talk of a regional Federation. Regional leaders were trying to educate the masses about the shift to this new political arrangement amidst a climate of intellectual debate about the advantages and disadvantages of the move. Beryl's twenty-seven-year-old existence seemed so far removed from that banter because no one in her family spoke of politics or even cared really.

Black Indian Mas
1955

CHAPTER TWO

All About Beryl

Beryl was a strange amalgam of various ideas that created a truly colourful personality. She was quiet but hyper-observant and had developed a passive aggressive nature to deal with her environment. She wore only black for two and a half years after her husband's death. Colours then seemed too extreme, so she wore white. She stayed close to Ma, raising her child and nursing her broken heart. Her world was far from insulated as she had been a witness to stories and all her siblings departure from the nest, until she was the only one left. The neighbourhood responded to her in a gentle way, after all, she was 'poor Beryl'. The most compelling reason to change her actions was still little Thomas. He was seven years old before she decided to enter into another relationship. Junior saw her shopping in San Fernando one day and he tried to approach her. Things did not go so well that first encounter but over the next six months he would be persistent until they started talking regularly. Beryl never agreed to go anywhere with Junior unchaperoned until after about nine months she agreed that he could visit her at home to meet her mother. Things progressed quickly after that, and by June 1961, Beryl was married again.

Junior was a short, brown skinned, man of African descent who had a serious outlook on life. He worked at Tyre Services Ltd. and led a simple life. Pursuing Beryl brought him out of his comfort zone a bit, because he was convinced that he could build something with her. The birth of Beryl's second child, Jeremy, came in April 1962. The family grew. She stayed at home with the kids and Junior worked to support the family. The marriage was far from ideal. Junior was withdrawn most times and always angry, not necessarily with Beryl, but always angry. Apparently some earlier trauma in his life made him an odd sort. These traits were only revealed after. The main source of conflict was the relationship between Thomas and his mother. Junior thought that Beryl sheltered the boy too much, pandered to his wants, defended him too much. It seemed to him that she was over compensating for the loss of his father. Thomas was now eight years old. He asked a lot of questions, had a lot of energy and only had his mother to play with. Early in the marriage, it was clear that Junior did not have patience for children.

The passage of time brought clarity to Junior as he realised that he never really got Beryl. She was still in love with the idea of a dead man whose shoes he could not fill. Beryl's passive-aggressive nature was also starting to push conflict into the zone of physical confrontation. Junior would only pay attention to Jeremy while ignoring Thomas. He was a hardworking man but soon realised that he was not happy in his marriage. He was not accustomed being happy anyway and most people said marriage was hell, so he resigned himself to his fate. Although he had no interest in politics, on occasion he attended meetings after work in San Fernando where speakers presented their arguments for Independence from the British Crown. The national narrative had shifted from Federation to Independence but Junior did not care, there were people to work that out. He would stand in the back of the crowd and listen. On occasion, after work, he would go out with co-workers to a bar. None of these things were really his thing but he did not want to go home. Junior did not need much, he was a simple man but angry all the time, and now he resented his wife for using him, but they continued to live like this for some time.

Beryl had her hands full with her two boys but that was the easy part, as long as Junior was not around. The atmosphere of the house changed when he came home. She knew how to stay out of his way but Thomas was not as skilled as she was. Thomas became tense and guarded and always on edge around Junior. The spankings were particularly aggressive and Beryl could not protect him all the time. She knew that everything she was doing was for her children and her sacrifice was worth it but sometimes things got out of control.

Thomas had developed seemingly normally over the years and seemed to be an average child. He was actually an underachiever though. His natural ability pulled him through as he never actually applied himself to most tasks. He had developed a passion for drawing and made use of his lonely moments by doodling on paper. Thomas got through primary school and started secondary school in Fyzabad, a short commute away. Fyzabad Intermediate Secondary School was quite an adjustment for him and he had to quickly mature to settle into his new situation. The additional financial demands were a challenge for Beryl because she knew that her husband was paying for Thomas' education and she really tried not to 'rock the boat'. He gave silently but it was a subject of reproach during arguments.

Things came to a head when Thomas was fourteen years old. One day he came home with a letter from the school requesting a meeting with his parents about the days he was absent and late. Beryl was in a dilemma about what Junior's reaction would be. She worried about the reason for his absence on some days when there was no money. He found the letter before she she could figure out how to approach him. In anger he lunged at Thomas but Beryl got in the way and what happened next just got out of hand. Junior punched Beryl twice and knocked her to the floor, Thomas picked up a bottle from the table and threw it at his stepfather hitting him in the face. Junior was taken completely aback as Thomas never showed signs that he could ever do that. Junior took Thomas' school bag and emptied the contents in the bathroom and turned on the shower, completely soaking the books. He went into a rant about his money being spent to raise an ungrateful child and it ended with him telling Beryl that Thomas could not stay in his house any more. Beryl took her son to stay with her mother that evening. She sat next to Ma and she cried, everything was falling apart and she did not know what to do.

Beryl returned home to Junior knowing that he was not the kind of man to change his mind, she felt that Junior had always planned to get rid of Thomas. He was not a forgiving man and he was getting worse. Her face still swollen, she vowed that he would never get to hit her again. She left within two weeks. she took Jeremy while Junior was at work and she went to live with her mother who then lived with her eldest son. When he came home and found an empty house, Junior knew exactly where she had gone. He was not surprised and in a way relieved. The tension in his life was finally over. No more wondering when it would end. This was it, this was the end.

CHAPTER THREE

Progress

Social revolution swept through Thomas' family when he was fifteen. His aunt, Beryl's little sister, helped them to get an apartment in La Romaine. Beryl was thirty-eight years old and had to get a job to support her children. She applied to be a domestic for an old white woman in Vistabella. No one wanted to work for the old woman but Beryl took the job. For the first time she would be really stepping out on her own to rent and take care of her children with the promise of assistance from her sister. She got to move in to the apartment after only paying her first month's rent because her brother-in-law was related to the owner of the house. It was a four dwelling apartment house with a separate structure in the north-western side of the property. Banana trees lined the western side of the property. The tenants had two shared facilities, the stand pipe in the yard and the outhouse on the north-eastern side of the property. The landlord was a hardworking man and he always kept the surroundings tidy. It was amazing that by six am in the morning when everyone was stirring, he was almost finished cutting the grass.

Ma's last child, Cathleen, possessed all the characteristics of being the youngest in a group of siblings. She was selfish, judgemental and aggressive, as though she took none of the examples of her mother. She performed poorly at school, and so was lucky to secure her school leaving certificate. At sixteen she helped at a kindergarten. She was seven years younger than Beryl and moved through life with three times the speed and five times the needs. She liked clothes and shoes and wanted to do all the popular things. Thank God Ma still had some kind of control over her environment and two sons to keep Cathleen in line. Cathleen was not shy, neither with boys nor with life, and at twenty when she brought Michael home to meet Ma, she was eager to leave the nest. Michael described her as lightening in a bottle but he was drawn to her energised spirit. Ma asked Michael at some point if he was sure about Cathleen as she knew that her daughter could be a handful but he said that she was the one. They were married in 1958, two years after Cathleen introduced him to her mother. They moved into Michael's sister's house in 1962 when she migrated to the United States.

La Romaine, like most sub-urban areas, developed slowly moving from only residential structures lining the main road to small businesses like shops, a bar, small hardware and gas station popping up. Residential developments occurred on a few side streets but the bulk of the land to the east of the main road, behind the residential plots, were used for agriculture, mostly sugar cane. The area drew people from rural areas looking for work but also gave haven to the persons from the town looking for cheaper rental options. This area started to build in popularity through community cultural activities like their Best Village performances and with tournaments in stick fighting in the lead up to the Carnival season. This promoted a feeling of pride and because the area was large, there was no shortage of talented persons in different disciplines. Activities were also common as the community fed a lively appetite for entertainment.

Thomas had arrived in a growing residential setup at the right time and the right age to see all the changes that this community would go through. It would grow as he grew and he would be in the eye of the storm. The wider climate in Trinidad was being influenced by international and regional events. Two years after the death of U.S. Civil Rights movement leader, Dr. Martin Luther King Jr. and in the wake of the strong statements by Kwame Ture about how local blacks should use their power and organise to reclaim an identity, the country was tense and ripe for controversy by 1970. Early 1970 saw University students protesting in the capital city and the National Joint Action Committee declaring "Black Power" in Trinidad and Tobago. Thomas was one of those youths with their heads in the sand. His awareness only peaked listening to his uncle's rantings about the socio-political climate. This climate didn't affect him much.

He was a happy youth for the first time. He made friends, had the support of his aunt and was mentored by her husband. Sixteen-year-old Thomas developed interests in cycling, drawing and jogging through the cane fields with friends. The whole area became their playground.

CHAPTER FOUR

Teen Bliss

1971 found Thomas settled into his community, knowing his way around and being acquainted with the neighbours. Seventeen is a complicated time. You are not really old enough to meddle in grown folks' business but you are exposed to most general occurrences. Cathleen had three children by now and used Thomas to help with their care. This led to tension between the two sisters. Beryl observed that Cathleen used Thomas to help with her obligations while not paying attention to how they affected Thomas. His schooling was one such area, where Cathleen had no problem with Thomas walking her boys to primary school while not attending his school due to various excuses that Thomas and his aunt would cook up. Yes, money was an issue but Thomas abused the situation as well. The arrangement was very laxed for Thomas as he was home alone with his brother during the week and the neighbours would 'throw an eye' while Beryl was gone to work. Thomas never took looking after Jeremy as his responsibility, so that task really fell to the neighbours. Beryl felt concerned that Thomas had a vested interest in the activities of Cathleen's children but not his little brother. Jeremy hated to visit Cathleen's house because he did not feel welcome. Cathleen was a strange sort, as she had no problem with showing her displeasure to a child because she did not like his father. She never forgave Junior for the abuses to her sister.

The climate contributed to Thomas' mediocre performance at the General Certificate of Education examinations. This was a British exam that marked the penultimate event in Thomas' secondary school life, but he did not care much. Thomas had become more of a creative type who liked working with his hands. He rationalised that his mother did not have money to send him to university anyway so he was content with the results. His reading and writing skills were good and he was sharp, he would get by. The close of the year found him occupied with a secret passion. November opened with the area steel band bringing out their steel drums and starting their preparations for the Carnival season. The secret activity was secret, only because he could not let Beryl know that he was involved in anything to do with Carnival. She was still traumatised by the death of his father. Cathleen was a Carnival baby though, and she said that it was in their blood. She covered for Thomas as he slipped away for pan practice with his cousin. Thomas and his cousin were close, but while his cousin played for three bands in different areas, Thomas only played in La Romaine. The community too, kept his secret. When Beryl was away for work, the boys practiced in the yard, especially for 'pan round the neck' events. People did not mind the noise because they played well and they were good boys who never got into any trouble. Thomas was good at that, you could never point a finger at him and make the obvious statement about him, he always tried to appear blameless. Thomas tried to maintain the persona of an exemplar.

These boys were typical red-blooded young males who were distracted by the presence of females. The girls liked Thomas and found him respectful, good looking, helpful and flattering to them. He developed romantic relationships with some but hid that from his mother. Hiding things from Beryl became a norm. Lots of people did it as she seemed to develop the reputation for being eccentric and a hard-line pragmatic figure in the community.

Thomas developed a little network for himself. He had a girlfriend who lived on the main road, just opposite the gas station and a girl from school who would visit him at home from time to time and the strangest arrangement of all, in the same yard where he lived, there was a young Indian girl who had been adopted by one of his neighbours, Thomas formed a relationship with her that was loosely defined but enduring. She saw some of his girlfriends visiting and never cared once she had his attention when they were gone. In a way, she got the best deal as he lived there and she saw him the most.

Young love, the folly of youth or blind infatuation, this was the time for it and the environment delivered it in spades.

La Romaine was adequate for Thomas the teenager, but adulthood had other plans instore for him. His father's brother would occasionally enquire about him whenever he saw Beryl. When he turned eighteen, he made a special effort to seek out Thomas and invite him to visit his home. The first thing Thomas saw as he walked through the door was a picture of his father on the wall. It was a black and white picture which clearly depicted his father's characteristic smooth black skin and wavy jet-black hair. It was a head shot to end all head shots. His uncle asked him if he recognised the person in the picture and Thomas could only nod in affirmation. His uncle told him that although Beryl never spoke about his father, she loved him very much and this picture had to be taken away from her because she would just sit and stare at it for hours. His uncle said that it was time to know about the Celestine family, the good, the bad and the ugly. They had been waiting to welcome him for a long time but a feud between Beryl and Thomas' grandmother made it impossible.

Thomas learned that his father had three surviving siblings and a lot of cousins, some close to his age and some much older. The real shock was meeting his grandmother who embraced him as though she had gotten her son back and she instantly declared him her favourite grandchild. Thomas was concerned that the other grandchildren would be jealous but to his surprise, they did not seem to care. They later told him that she had started to experience bouts of forgetfulness and could be talking to someone one minute and forget the topic mid-sentence. He observed in amazement as the household operated as everyone took turns watching Granny because when she was unsupervised, she would just walk away. Living on the fourth floor of a building helped, as she had to make it down eight flights of stairs before she could make it to the court yard and a neighbour raise the alarm. He also met an aunt living in another building in Pleasantville just ten minutes away, if you were walking. Everyone stayed away from her, but she too accepted Thomas with open arms. Her kids were even stranger than the other set of cousins. This was a lot to take in, so much change all at once, and everyone praising his father's memory and talking about how good he was.

Having three buildings on one piece of land, with so many people living together, was so far removed from what he knew was somewhat overwhelming. His cousins kept him close and protected him. He soon got to meet everyone. His female cousins had friends who lived in the buildings, this meant that there were intrigues with girls and his male cousins were respected in their little community so there was no conflict with the guys. Thomas was comfortable, he could come and go as he pleased in what some thought was a rough part of the neighbourhood. It took some time but he got comfortable. He sometimes stayed for a couple of weeks at a time, and they were always glad to have him because as they put it, he was family. There was a young woman in his grandmother's building, whose family was close to his family. She was light skinned and beautiful and the eldest of three sisters. A mutual attraction existed from the first time they met. He would be a fool to not notice her, She was among the most beautiful of the girls in the buildings. This motivated many visits to his grandmother.

Sisters

CHAPTER FIVE

Growing Pains

The Best Village competition was second only to the Steel band as a community cultural activity. The Community Center came alive with drums and singing. Well-known folk songs rang out most evenings in preparation for a series of events leading up to national finals. This is where Thomas first saw them. Two young ladies whose brother he knew but whom he rarely saw in the village. They seldom attended other events. This was their event though as they both had roles in the choir and participated in the dance segments. They were an odd pair. They were one year apart in age, but the younger sister was physically bigger than the elder sister but it was clear to see who was in charge. Thomas was drawn to the younger sister seemed more daring, reckless and rebellious compared to her older sibling. He was determined to get close to her and it would not have been very difficult as the girls knew him to be their brother's friend. May 1974 even saw Thomas take a more active part in the culture showcase by playing percussion devices, all to gain the attention of his newest romantic interest.

Ruth, the younger of the two sisters was a simple creature who hid the turmoil within her with an innocent smile and demure presence. It was difficult for one to not be drawn in by her because she seemed to be a mystery. Truth be known, she was a lonely girl who felt lost among eight siblings and abandoned by her parents. Her father had died when she was six years old and her mother had migrated to work leaving her to live with her siblings. She hated taking orders from her older brothers. She loved to have fun though, and when given the chance, gave in to gay abandon as though she had no cares in the world. What she lacked in life experience she made up for in bravery. She was at times fearless. Her sister was her rock for all other times. Strong and capable, focused and loyal, her sister stood tall in their household. Younger than the boys, but trusted by her mother, she was key to everyone's survival. Ruth noticed Thomas and gave him opportunities to talk to her. She had never been interested in boys before but she noticed Thomas. He was a man. The four-year difference between them made him seem mature and worldly. She wondered why he seemed to be interested in talking to her, but she liked the attention and secretly she liked the idea that he chose her and not her sister. They had noticed each other, and they knew that their story had only just started to unfold.

The busy environment was perfect for a secret courtship. They thought it was secret, but others noticed. Having a few outings to neighbouring villages meant that they spent a little time together. When the activities ended, all they had was a chance encounter on public transport or the rare visit to her house to hang out with her brother and friends. It was a nice challenge for Thomas but even as things grew dormant there were other entanglements that demanded his attention. When Thomas doubted his ability to figure out the opposite sex, Joeleen always came to mind. She lived on the main road in La Romaine and she had known Thomas for almost as long as he lived in their area. She was a year older than Thomas and was always talking about her plans to leave Trinidad. She had family in the United states and planned to migrate. She liked Thomas, and as close as they were, he always held back because he knew that one day she world leave. She also had a domineering personality and he hated being managed, but he liked Joeleen despite her flaws primarily because she spoiled him with gifts and surprises and they were each other's first - a secret that belonged to them that helped strengthen their bond. She was a free agent though. Her family usually had suitors in mind for her and she entertained them as she was expected to. Thomas knew that they could not announce their relationship because he didn't have a good job and could not compete with the family's idea of a suitor, so they were what they were, good friends with secrets.

That year ended and with the new, came excitement and anticipation. Carnival was always anticipated, but after it was over, the Best Village preparation started. Two people especially looked forward to this year's participation, knowing that this was time that they could spend together. Thomas and Ruth took full advantage of this time, talking, catching up on the past year and declaring feelings for each other. They even got the opportunity to stroll away from practice a couple of times so that Thomas could show her where he lived. Things progressed at a nice slow pace, Thomas knew she was scared to do anything that would get her brothers upset, he was patient with her. This made her feel safe with him and she trusted him. Her sister and one of her brothers found out about what was developing with Thomas. This was not a bad thing though as they kept the secret.

Letters and chance encounters seemed harder this time once the regular meetings had ceased. School had finished early one day in late November and Ruth was determined to see Thomas, she stopped short of her destination and walked into his street to see if he was home but she had missed him. She left a message with his neighbour that she had tried to visit. He was both glad and upset at the same time but the surprise was that she was willing to risk getting in trouble to see him. He wondered if something was wrong. The next day he found an excuse to go visit her brother and he got an opportunity to speak with Ruth. He left there determined to put more effort into their relationship and find a way for them to spend time together. He had begun getting sucked into her world not realising that her needy emotional behaviour came from more than just her attraction to him. They would meet after school and commute home together. Sometimes she left school early and visited him at his home. The second time

Ruth tried to visit Thomas, she had not arrived long when Beryl came home early. Beryl lost it when she saw Ruth in her house in a school uniform. She told him that he would spoil the people's girl child and that he was no good and she warned them both that what they were doing would end poorly. The walk home was sombre, but Thomas told Ruth that everyone thought that his mother was eccentric and no one took her seriously. They would just have to be more careful next time.

Early December came and Ruth cut school to spend an entire day with Thomas. She was totally committed to the plan, although this would be more time than they had ever spent together before. She was a little nervous. She noticed that he was a lot more direct than usual. He was very physical and not as patient as she remembered. She asked him to slow down and confessed that she was scared because of all the warnings that she received from everybody. Thomas told her that everything would be ok. He said that he knew what he was doing and that she could relax. Ruth was tense as she had never had sex before. It was not even a topic that she and her sister would discuss, but she liked Thomas and she did not want him to be upset with her. She was conscious of her body while taking her clothes off and curious about his. Then suddenly a rush of panic came over her and she had to stop. She could not do this. She started to dress again. Thomas held her and calmed her down. He told her that he loved her, that he needed her and wanted her for a long time. He promised her that this is what people in love do and as a couple they would be stronger after. Ruth really needed to hear that he loved her and she relaxed, giving in to the sex act. Ruth noted the discomfort and was grateful that the experience did not take very long. She lay clutched against Thomas as though she would never let him go. She felt free from her siblings and just in that moment, nothing else mattered.

Beryl found out about Thomas's entertaining a female for the entire day, and once again, lost it. This ordinarily quiet woman could really cause a ruckus when she wanted to, and now she wanted to. Thomas, realising that things were about to get really frustrating for him, decided to spend some time at his father's family home in Pleasantville. He would wait for this to blow over. He sent word to Ruth about what happened, she would miss him but she was glad that she did not get into any trouble on her end. He was off to avoid his mother and the change of pace was always a good idea. He had fun with his cousins.

Weeks rolled by as Ruth replayed her secret day with her secret love while Thomas moved on to other distractions. Their worlds were separate and kept him thoroughly busy. He came back home just before Christmas because it was his favourite time of the year for his aunt's baking and cooking and the little odd jobs in the neighbourhood that ensured that he had money at the close of the year. He was so busy that even though she knew he was back, he had not been to see her. This was also the time when steel bands started practicing. Full days and nights meant that Thomas coordinated very little other than his main activities. The only communication between them was a few letters back and forth through Ruth's brother where Thomas tried to explain his absence. Ruth took ill in February and her sister took her to the doctor. The diagnosis paralysed them both. Ruth was pregnant. Her secret was now out. Her sister looked at her in disbelief. She quickly thought of her mother and brothers and then composed herself. She took her sister to a park they loved and sat on a bench and asked her everything. She knew she had to manage all of this just right or it could ruin everything and everyone. She felt responsible, but with no yelling and no panic, she would fix this. When they got home they told only one brother whose job it was to get Thomas to the house at a time of their choosing. Thomas could not understand the sense of urgency but he knew that Ruth was overdue for a visit, so he agreed.

Thomas arrived to find a sombre, sobbing Ruth, paralysed by fear of his reaction. Her siblings gave her the space to make the announcement. She finally told him that she was pregnant. He froze. He looked at her for a while, and when he could speak again, he told her that they would handle it. Her siblings came up with a plan. They estimated that she had about three weeks before she started showing so they could keep the secret a little while longer - until they would have to tell her big brothers and ultimately, her mother.

CHAPTER SIX

Honourable Intention

Thomas was accustomed to secrecy but this one was over his head. It taxed him to the core. It signalled the end of the road. There was no wiggle room. He had to break his rule of keeping Beryl in the dark. Their strange relationship seemed stronger. The first person he could think to tell his mother. She would fix it. He sheepishly blurted it out. He said he was in trouble and he needed her advice. The "I told you so" speech was inevitable but they quickly moved on to solutions. She had to be filled in on everything. She needed to know the lay of the land; who was involved and who knew. She asked him what he was willing to do. This didn't help. He was in a mess. She consoled her son and told him that things would work out, but she needed to speak to Ruth. He did not know if he could arrange it, but his mother pressed the issue.

With the help of her siblings, Ruth was able to get out to meet with Thomas and his mother. She was a sobbing, shaking mess but she was clear that she was in love and she wanted to keep her baby. She admitted that Thomas gave her something to drink to get rid of the pregnancy and she would not do that again. She fully expected Thomas to stand by her and take care of her and the baby. Beryl asked her if she knew what that meant, if she was ready for marriage and life away from home with a man. For the first time, Ruth realised that this was a path out of what she knew and not a downside. She said yes, she wanted to get married. There was no need for further questions. It was final. He felt trapped, but he agreed anyway. Her brothers still had to be told.

When the time was deemed right, Ruth's sister approached three of her older brothers for a meeting and gave them the news. There was the expected shock and consternation, blame assigning and panic. They also argued about who would tell their mother. Nobody wanted that task, so naturally it fell to her favourite, Ruth's sister. They agreed though, that they would have to go see this boy and find out what his intentions were with their sister and so it had begun, events set in motion that would change lives forever.

Ruth's brothers wasted no time, they inquired about the address and they visited in the evening. They called out and Beryl came out. They asked for Thomas and she told them that he was not at home. They told her about the reason for their visit and she informed them that she was aware of the situation and that she had spoken to her son and their sister and that they intended to do the honourable thing. She said that her son fully intended to stand by their sister and was willing to marry her. They left without any acrimony and now they had something to report to their matriarch. Phone conversations with their mother were rough because this threatened to destabilise everything that she had set up. She was selfish and narcissistic and things had to conform to her plan. Leaving her three-month-old son for her two daughters to raise seemed the perfect solution but this latest incident seemed an inconvenience to her. Ruth's opportunity to speak with her mother came with great trepidation, as the words could hardly leave her mouth. Her mother asked her if she wanted to migrate with her and have her son abroad but Ruth said no, she wanted to get married and be with Thomas. He mother's disappointment was followed by nonchalance. Ruth had made her bed and now she would lie in it.

Ruth had stopped school just before attempting her final examinations and was home adjusting to her pregnancy and sharing some of her sister's responsibilities. It was like seeing her sister for the first time, she was so efficient at most things and made things look so easy. The unexpected side effect of things being in the open was that now Thomas could come to her and bring things for her. He would find out what she needed and when he visited he tried to assist. He sister accompanied her to doctor visits and when she grew close to term, arrangements were made for midwives to come to the house and deliver her baby. It was in mid-September 1976 that she gave birth to a healthy seven-and-a-half-pound baby boy. He changed her life as she realised that now she had someone to take care of. Midwives can do that to you, drumming in your head key statements that train young mothers. She could not wait to show Thomas his son.

The news of the child's birth created a weighty moment in his life and he had the whole journey over to turn it around in his head. Finally, he arrived at the house and Ruth proudly extended her arms to give him his child. He froze. He did not know how to hold it. They spent some minutes showing him how to hold the baby, then he just sat there staring at the child. Within that moment, the child gave him purpose, things all seemed so real then. His responsibility was now becoming clear. He sat looking at the child's eye brows, hands and feet and he would pick which features that the baby got from his mother and the features that came from him. He wondered if his father had felt this proud the first time they met. He knew what had to happen now. It was the right thing to do for his son.

Three and a half months later Thomas and Ruth knelt before an Anglican Minister as they presented themselves to be wed. She was seventeen and he was twenty-one. The affair was a small gathering of only family. Only Ruth's mother was absent as she could not return from abroad. Thomas stood there in his burgundy bell bottom suit with his jet-black afro, while Ruth stood next to him, radiant like an angel in her white dress and veil holding her baby in her arms. They swore that day before God and man and their child to honour their holy union. After the service the couple took their guests back to their new home, an apartment downstairs Beryl, where they had refreshments and received blessings for their new life together. This part was of great importance to Ruth as this was a big step for one so young. She moved straight from her mother's house to her husband's house, but she was here, and this is where she would build a family for her son.

CHAPTER SEVEN

Trapped

Married at seventeen is never a seamless prospect, but for Ruth there were positive outcomes to focus on. It was the end of the old, stifling arrangements where she was issued orders and had to follow. No more being lost in the house where everyone else was more important. She hated picking up after grown men while they did nothing. She hated feeling trapped, with no idea of when it would end. Ruth had a habit of thinking in absolute terms and amalgamating her problems. Her new situation offered much and she was a willing participant to these changes. Her positive outlook was not enough to help her with the challenges of having a four month old to take care of and a husband to live with and cook for. She was pleasantly surprised that she got help from Beryl and the other female tenants in the yard and she learned quickly how to take care of her child as he grew. Her cooking though, was horrible. Thomas never expected her to be good at it but he had hoped that she would improve with time. Ruth went out of her way to observe her husband's likes and dislikes but inevitably made all the rookie mistakes, but she tried to learn from them. She was extremely sharp that way.

She had not anticipated the hardships that came with entering his world. Everyone around her cared about his feelings and what he wanted. This created an imbalance in the relationship. She began to realise that her new husband was extremely self-centred and bull-headed. He never listened to her or sought her opinion. Their relationship became tenuous. She was frustrated that she could not please him. He never complimented her and she felt unappreciated. She found solace in her child. He needed her and gave her the only source of unconditional love that she would get in this situation. Things were not all bad though, because there was always the sex. She would wonder if sex alone would make a marriage work, because thus far, that seemed to be the only area that she got right.

She loved how he would touch her and she imagined that his excitement meant that he really loved her and they had a strong bond. She never denied him, and she even learned to anticipate when he wanted to be sexual with her. She learned that sex was for him and even learned the things that he liked and did them energetically, willingly and lovingly. She knew that he was satisfied because of the things he did to her and the way she felt. She made excuses for his emotional inconsistency and took responsibility for their relationship.

Thomas had a very different orientation to married life. The apartment that he was given was arranged by Beryl and he felt that living downstairs his mother was not his idea of freedom. He was coerced to get married and now, sentenced to be beholden to his mother for an unacceptable period of time. The rent was seventy-five dollars a month plus he had to get items for the baby. His income was not constant. He made ends meet by doing labourer stints at the local roofing company, odd jobs and selling his craft. Thomas had become a skilled string-art craftsman. This form of art, made from using small nails, coloured string or thread and stencils to recreate pictures of trains, birds, faces for example on a wooden background was quite popular. He had sold quite a number of pieces. His new wife loved to watch him work in silence and she did not disturb him. There were some positives though. Ruth's mother lived abroad and sometimes sent items for the baby and money for her daughter.

The presence of his son also motivated Thomas. The child had lived apart from his father for four months and then he found himself standing over the child, staring. He was speechless, feeling full of something he was not sure of. Most times he renewed his commitment to do whatever it took to keep this little guy safe. He would not fail. He could not fail because he knew what it was like growing up without a father. He tried being patient with his new bride but she could not cook to save her life. Luckily, he still ate a lot by his aunt down the street and the baby needed only breastmilk.

His aunt's husband was a strong male influence in his life. He helped him find work and, on occasion, hired him to do odd jobs and bought pieces of his string art. Thomas was always lucky when it came to family support. They spoiled him in a way, but he learned to use every advantage that he could. He was also a fan of the sex. He usually found himself looking at her and remembering why he originally chose her. She was beautiful and sexy and had smooth skin. Despite the politics of their union, this outcome gave him the upper hand. He liked teaching her new things. He liked seeing the look on her face and she soon surpassed even his expectations. When life gives you lemons, you make lemonade. They would make this work, they had to.

CHAPTER EIGHT

FAMILY

One year into the marriage found Thomas in a strange and unexpected place. Although he was a restless soul and had many regrets by now, he had settled in somewhat to his new life. The joy of watching his son, now almost a year and a half, kept him cheerful. The child was smart and healthy, and the one thing that both Ruth and Thomas agreed upon was that he should have the best. This level of family living was altered though, by the news that Ruth was pregnant again. Thomas did not know how to receive the news, now he had just gotten a handle on the requirements of a family of three. To his credit though, he kept his comments to himself and allowed his wife the opportunity to prepare for her second pregnancy.

The strange thing was that Thomas was not around for the first pregnancy, so this was like his first. He got to see the sick phases, vomiting and weight gain, moodiness and the appetite adjustments. At times, it seemed too much. He wasn't really one to enjoy doctor's visits, so if someone else could stand in, he welcomed that.

This gave the perfect opening for Ruth's sister to step back into the picture, big-time. Although Ruth had friends in the neighbourhood, the best candidate for this kind of support was her sister. Coincidentally, Ruth's sister was also pregnant at this time, and although it came as a kind of shock to both to be pregnant at the same time, they enjoyed sharing that experience. The women made it almost a spiritual crusade to be there for each other and share the responsibility of looking out for their little brother who was now four and a half years old. Ruth's sister had grown so much in the past year. She was never one to be interested in men, but now there was someone in her life. Ruth had met him, she was not a fan, but she loved her sister and understood that she was stepping out of her comfort zone to try to do something different. Ruth supported her sister and enjoyed the support that she got in return.

The scene at home was much different now as their oldest brother had joined the Coast Guard and was spending most of his time in North Trinidad. Two of the other older brothers had moved out, one to an uncle in Port-of-Spain and the other got an apartment and launched his independence. This left only two male siblings in the house with Ruth's sister.

She was the middle child but she had all the power. Breaking the news to their mother about the pregnancy would have been easy, but the mother was a pragmatist. The mother realised that the situation at home was unravelling, but she went with it knowing that she could do nothing about it. She blamed Ruth in a way. Since Ruth's fall from grace, everything deteriorated after that. The mother was a survivor. Ruth visited home regularly and saw the rising tensions between her siblings. The oldest male left was very selfish and possessive. She tried to help where she could, to bring balance to conflict, but she was really supporting only her sister.

These visits were necessary as Ruth usually received a bounty of foodstuff that she took home to help with her family's situation. On that piece of land, that measured a mere lot and a half, there were five varieties of avocado, banana, plantain, cassava, guava, pumpkin, pigeon peas, sorrel, dasheen, plants that could be brewed for tea substitutes, medicinal plants for treating the common cold, sugar cane stalks at the back, caraillee (bitter melon) passion fruit and barbadine vines on the fence and soursop. When she came home to Trinidad, Ruth's mother made tropical wines from hibiscus and the various fruits that she could find. Lots of the fruits in the yard came directly from Grenada and were preserved in that space. Many days it saved the lives of Ruth and her family. She would always be grateful for her parents' foresight.

Ruth, being the first to launch out in life, and possibly because she was the youngest girl, her mother made her an offer to allow her to build on a parcel of land that she owned in La Romaine, which was not too far from the house where Ruth had grown up. Thomas and Ruth liked the idea and started clearing the land and preparing it for construction. This was the signal to Ruth's eldest brother still occupying the house, to act. He started cultivating the land and claimed that they were destroying his crops. Rather than let the conflict grow, Thomas told his wife that they would leave the land for him.

Ruth complied but she would not forget her brother's act of greed and sabotage. She knew going to her mother was futile as she was not physically here to keep the tyrant in line. Housing for Ruth's family would not come in this way. The twenty-minute walk between Ruth's apartment and her mother's property was possible up until about eight months into her pregnancy, after which she was confined to home. This period was particularly difficult as she started having powerful stomach contractions. Her stomach would get distended and darkened. She was sometimes in a lot of pain. Beryl was a life line here as she took over supervising Ruth's health. Ruth's sister had troubles of her own. It was a circus when Ruth finally went into labour. Midwives came to the house and Beryl was front centre. Ruth had been in labour for most of the day and she had complications. The umbilical cord was tied around the child's neck and the midwives could not deliver the baby. At the height of Ruth's exhaustion and the midwives' frustration, Beryl asked if she could try. Beryl bolstered Ruth's courage, altered her position and told her that the pain was to save her child's life. Beryl managed to turn the baby and the child crowned and came out blue and with cord around its neck, but when the midwife slapped it, it yelled out with a powerful voice. It was another boy. Ruth never expected Beryl to do that for her. They had a moment.

Naturally, Thomas would not want to see his wife laid out suffering in labour. He waited upstairs for Beryl to bring the news. Even then he waited for the midwives to clear out and only came down to see his second son after they were cleaned up. All was well with mother and child. Thomas was grateful because he really hated bad news. In his life he never prepared his mind for bad news. It was not that he was an optimist but rather that he just could not deal with bad news. He would fall to pieces, need consoling and had to rely on strong persons around him who did not have a similar reaction to bad news. This was Beryl most times, overcompensating for conditions long past. This was a good day though, and as he held his second son for the first time, he felt even more attached to this child.

That year's end saw Ruth as a mother of two and an aunt of two children as both her sister and brother became parents. Their lives were changing rapidly but they resolved to stay close to each other. Support was now critical as they charted a new course into their respective futures.

Mas Costume

San Fernando
Mid. 1950's

CHAPTER NINE

Tempered Glass

Life nudged Thomas along. Sometimes gently and sometimes with the urgency necessary to match changes in the environment. He could not recognise his life, married with two children. This time, even he had to pause to look at the implication of his new situation. Without any prodding he knew that he needed a steady income, but these thoughts were not coming in a vacuum. He had developed a plan for his future that involved joining the Police Force. The plan came with friends who had already started studying for the entrance examination. Thomas applied himself to these tasks and was determined to apply. 1979 found him settling into this reality a bit more and relatives noticed changes in him.

The community was changing as the relationship with the police was worsening because of foot pursuits and raids on specific groups of youths who were bringing drugs into the area. It might even be interesting to accept that, as Thomas made moves to align himself with the police, his brother aligned himself with the drug dealing criminal characters. This would become yet another source for conflict between the brothers. Both were myopic in their view of the world and the bigger picture was lost on them.

Trinidad at that time was a place of conflicting ideals and blame for political and regional positions on matters. Our socialist/capitalist hybrid economy caused various responses from scholars and citizens working the systems alike. The citizens still didn't have a clear picture of how the model worked. Most didn't care, but Thomas' uncle paid close attention. Though he was not an academic he represented a type of citizen that the 1950's tried to build. Someone with a stake in their country's future. The only way he exercised this stake though was through his chain link fence to his neighbour. However it served to give the younger persons some kind of second hand perspective about most things. Social commentary was never far as calypsos were always telling stories of the day and 'ole mas' in carnival would remind us of recent events. Yet still Thomas' generation got by on just the barest essentials and little more.

Ruth witnessed this transformation, as her husbands' homely outlook changed to a kind of outward focusing personality. He worried more and though their relationship had not developed to a stage where they openly spoke about things, she had gotten really good at reading him. It was not too difficult a skill as he usually purged when he was upset but now was even different. He kept certain plans close to his chest and only confided in Beryl. Beryl helped him focus on preparing for his entrance exam and though she was no scholar, she was pretty sharp when it came to current affairs and general social studies material. Thomas was surprised because he had never looked at his mother as that type of knowledgeable person. They both gained from the interaction.

Ruth was a housewife, but even her responsibilities were increasing. Both her children were breastfeeding and she tried to help more with the supervision of her little brother as her sister had a new born to care for and this was her first. Her brother was now five and their mother was back, so she enrolled him into a primary school in San Fernando. The sisters would have to coordinate these changes that their mother implemented once she left again. Thomas paid little mind to Ruth's visits to her mother's house. Ruth learnt that telling him less was best because his comments were seldom kind and after the land business, he had reason to be bitter. The only relative that really visited was Ruth's little brother and Thomas had no problems with that. There were times when the boys played noisily or engaged in mischief, like cutting each other's hair with scissors, but Ruth was allowed to handle that and deal out punishment. They lived simple frugal lives and somehow family was at the core of most of their dealings. They took the good with the bad and got by.

September of that year, Thomas joined the group of trainees that started at the Police Training Facility in St James. It was the proudest day of his life. His uncle drove him up and the whole family bid him farewell as he was expected to be in training for months. His bags packed, Beryl ensured that he had everything that was on his list. It was up to him now. 'South boy come to town to show them what he was made of'. The emotions of the day could not be contained. Everyone made sacrifices within this period as Ruth rallied along with the help of Beryl and meagre resources were shared. Thomas came out one weekend every six weeks and when he got home, everyone put on a brave face and did nothing to stress him. He went back charged and ready to excel. He was not one to dote over children but in these times his thoughts fell on his boys and the future that he would build for them. Things were finally looking up for him and he had the world of plans but he never took his eyes off the prize. His training record, by his reckoning, was top draw and he pushed to keep it there.

Back home, all that was hidden played out in his absence, Ruth felt that she was surrounded by enemies as Thomas' mother, grandmother and aunt were viewed as a council of treacherous and deceitful women. Their words cut like knives and Ruth would take no criticism from them. She felt like she was constantly being watched and that she had no one in her corner. Suddenly everyone spoke of her husband in glowing terms and she had to be worthy of him. It was ridiculous because it was all a show but now fantasy was replacing her reality. Even when she tried to spend time away at her mother's house they found fault with her.

The return to training after Thomas' third weekend off was noteworthy. Having settled in, two weeks had passed before he was summoned to a meeting by the facility's administrators. He was not worried because he knew that his scores were good and he had been a model Cadet. He spoke with three officers in uniform, their demeanour serious and their authority evident by their posture and tone. They took no time explaining to him that he would not be allowed to continue training. This day was his last at the facility and he would return to his dorm and clear out his belongings and leave the facility. Thomas could not speak but the look on his face prompted further comments from the lead officer. He was told that he did not pass his vetting and that he could pursue other careers, but the police could not hire him. Ten minutes in that room changed his life forever. The walk from the dorm to the main road took a ridiculous amount of time as each step cemented a reality in a timeline that was not his. He should be in there but instead, he was here on the main road. Taxis were trying to get his attention to take him where? After he walked for an hour he ended up around the savannah in Port of Spain looking helpless. He thought to himself that this must be what rock bottom feels like, then he corrected himself, because he could feel nothing.

Two hours after the event found him on a park bench around the savannah but finally he started to gather his thoughts. He could not go home. Not like this. He could not face the disappointed looks on every face that he would meet and having to repeat the story. He would go to Pleasantville, he had not told them about his plans. With a destination in mind he got up and made his way to downtown Port of Spain, to secure conveyance to San Fernando. The long drive to San Fernando brought all the questions that the park bench suppressed. It was as if the closer he got to home the more real the whole thing became until at a certain point he could hardly breathe. Silently he sat in his seat trying to catch his breath. Heart pounding in his throat, he felt sick. Then, like a wave, it passed. He felt nothing again. His heart was breaking. His soul was crying for something that he had worked so hard for and it had been taken away. Why?!? He had no answer for this one-word question and it haunted him from the moment that he mustered the clarity of thought to ask it. It was like a black hole of questions that consumed him and allowed him to lose himself in the asking of it. Why?!?

Once in San Fernando, he took a taxi to Pleasantville where his arrival went largely unnoticed. He went upstairs, greeted his grandmother and settled in. As he had expected, he was welcomed there and there were few questions. He offered an explanation about having issues with his mother and this was all his grandmother wanted to hear. His cousins found him to be in poor spirits as they tried to involve him in their regular activities. Thomas even avoided his female friend who was usually the highlight of his visits. It took him two weeks before he worked up the courage to visit home. He was grateful for this time at relatives but he knew he could not run from this forever.

Early on Saturday morning Thomas arrived home and he went to Beryl. She was surprised to see him and instinctively knew something was wrong. He told his tale for the first time knowing that it would not be the last. Beryl was upset and naturally had a barrage of questions to which Thomas had no answers to. She swore to fight the decision, to protest, but Thomas was no longer where she was. He had come home to start the process of healing. His brother overheard the conversation and came out to give condolences. He was honest as well in saying that he thought it was for the best.

Thomas had not finished that discourse before he noticed his mother's face had changed. He knew the look well so he asked her what was wrong. She looked at him squarely in the face and told him that she believed that Ruth was pregnant and she apologised for being the one to tell him. Thomas was prepared for his version of coming home but he was not ready for this. He turned and left. He had to hear it from the source. Ruth was surprised to see him and before she could greet him, he asked her if she was pregnant. She froze, became speechless and all she could manage was a headshake in the affirmative. In that moment she saw before her a thoroughly broken man. He asked her who was the father, yet again she could not answer. He knew that it was not his. That he knew from the urgency of his mother's announcement. He turned and left, he could endure no more updates from home.

Chapter Ten

Last Decision

Thomas' life was unravelling at a blistering rate and he had to get his head sorted. To his credit it took one more week at his grandmother's house to construct his plan. He thanked his grandmother for allowing him to stay with them and as suddenly as he arrived, he departed. This time he went home to his wife and initiated a serious conversation in which he told her that he would give the child his name and they would press on with life. He had no interest in dragging this issue on and making things worse for everyone. Ruth agreed, though she was confused and was not expecting this outcome. She took the opportunity to 'move on'. Having made this decision, Thomas changed, became more private, secretive and bordered on being paranoid. He stayed indoors more. Avoided his mother and other family members. The real casualty of the new arrangement was the marriage. Things got really bad and they only spoke to address those routine issues attached to running a household, and the needs of the children. Thomas did not trust her and she could feel it every time they were forced to interact. Money was low and living was becoming increasingly difficult. Thomas slipped into this 'poor me' cocoon for about six months after returning home. He still held on to the hope that the injustice that had been done to him could be rectified. This faded in and out of his active thoughts while doing nothing to secure a future for himself. It took a visit to his uncle's house to snap him out of his stupor.

His uncle told him that he had no choice in being a man. He had to take care of himself first and only when a man was strong, could he care for others. He advised Thomas to go out into the world and get a job and build himself so that no one could look down their nose at him. He reminded him that Celestines don't quit and that his father was no quitter. This seemed to be the kick in the pants that Thomas needed because the next day he was looking for work. The strange thing was that when he assessed his capability, Thomas found that there was only one thing that he could do confidently. He looked around and asked around about Security Guard vacancies. It was not long before he found a company that serviced Government contracts for school security and maintenance. His interview went well, and they were impressed with his writing and comprehension skills. He got a job, a steady income and an opportunity to get his life back on track. This new development coincided with the birth of the third child and things were very different this time. Ruth relied heavily on her sister and the delivery was done at the San Fernando General Hospital. The child was born with bronchial problems and had to stay in the hospital for observation. Thomas skipped the entire affair and that should have served as a sign for things to come. The arrival of the third child in the household came with no fanfare and no one came to see him but he was a beautiful baby boy. Soon he would win over the hearts of all that met him except for one, whose mind had been made up for some time and whose thoughts conflicted with his promise.

The events of the past year changed Thomas significantly. More responsibility meant that his approach had to change. It was not long after getting settled that he started checking out the option of having Ruth work at the same company in the Maintenance section. This job required no qualification and there was on-the-job training. He spoke to Ruth about the idea and she was excited to have the opportunity to earn money and not be a burden. Early in 1981, Ruth applied for the job, was interviewed and was hired to work in a secondary school next to Thomas' place of work. This was an unexpected development but at least she had a job. Thomas was a shift worker while Ruth worked from eight to four, Mondays to Fridays, with her weekends off. This made them occupants of different worlds and their strained marriage could not improve under these circumstances. Thomas really did not care, he lost himself in his new-found freedom and Beryl was there to babysit in those times when needed.

Domestically the conflict between Ruth and Thomas changed. The new mix of circumstances added to an already volatile marriage. Thomas could not deal with the embarrassment he felt when he was around his family and his job came with its own set of stressors. Ruth had been enduring a surreal reception to her new job. Co-workers looked at her strangely and some shared rumours about her husband being involved with women in the school. There was no way to confirm these stories so they were best left alone. When Thomas was in a foul mood and Ruth did not feel to cower before him, things quickly escalated into a physical affair. He just had to land the first blow before she sprang into action to fight him. The past years had made her a worthy adversary. She matched him in height, had broader shoulders than him and a general weight advantage. She knew how to use these assets in a fight. Their fights would be short-lived because Beryl was never far, to rush to separate the two. It was barely a marriage any more but rather, waves of disappointment.

1981 was a particularly important year for Trinidadians. This was the year that they lost their first Prime Minister on 29th March. After nineteen years, now a new leader would have to be chosen to fill such big shoes. Eric Williams had many detractors but even more supporters and his accomplishments loomed large both locally and internationally. This year though was a year for yet another first. Thomas and Ruth's first born was beginning primary school. He would finally join his uncle to start a tradition at the school. The waves of change seemed to come that year as the two-bedroom apartment that the family subsisted in seemed to be too small. An option became available down the street. It was a house and the rent was six hundred dollars but the couple took it. The house was elevated on tall pillars, made of concrete with three bedrooms a large living room and a kitchen. It offered a paved area under the house for the children to play. The biggest detractor for the selection was that it was directly opposite Thomas' aunt's house. A world of conflict loomed.

The couple was on their own in this house. There was no Beryl to separate fights and the children witnessed everything, from the scuffles to the fact that the couple slept in separate rooms. Things quickly escalated with Thomas' aunt. Ruth solved that problem by banning her from the house, so the exchanges now took place across the street. Ruth learned to ignore that. What she could not ignore was her husband's mood swings which made it difficult to talk to him about progressive things. Debt and bills were particularly difficult to talk about because now that Ruth was working he left her to handle that. He contributed when he felt like it and that put a financial strain on both Ruth and the marriage. This period saw Thomas growing more and more independent and he lived like he had no dependants. His time was his and he had built up quite a network of friends both on and off the job. The social activity came to a halt when Thomas broke his leg during a football match at the company's Family Day. Strangely enough, his family was at home when Ruth got the call notifying her that he was in the hospital. When she brought him home, it was a sad day for Thomas. He was wearing a full leg cast and expected to be home for five months. He did not have to worry about his job but he had the rely on his wife.

Ruth was young but smart. She took care of him the way the doctors suggested, and she did not nag. Rather, for the first time she found that she had him all to herself. She still wanted to make their marriage work and she had been working hard to win his approval. Unfortunately, her faith in him was misplaced. He had moved on to a place where the marriage was about dominance and convenience. He was uncomfortable with the fact that she did so much for him and gratitude did not live in his heart. Something else dwelt there that usually blamed others for everything and twisted fact to absolve Thomas each time. During this time though payments grew stable. He could not go anywhere, and no one came to see him, so he paid bills with Ruth. The surreal feel of this period gave way to an unexpected closeness and for the first time in a long time, they acted like a family. Their fourth child was born. Ruth brought him home from the hospital to mixed reviews from her husband. Strange chap, he really liked children but the responsibility scared him every time. His leg had long since healed and he was back out there making up for lost time. He felt like his five-month term was a prison sentence. Now he had to live.

They were given a strange offer by the landlord. The house was for sale and the tenants were given the first option. It seemed like a big decision and the couple discussed it. Eventually though, the opportunity went the way of most dreams because Thomas just did not want to discuss things further. Mere months after the family failed to purchase the property, they would have to move to make way for the new owners.

CHAPTER ELEVEN

Hope

Contemplating a move now could only mean one thing. The couple agreed that the family's future hinged on leaving La Romaine. The area was fast becoming less safe and it was changing because of negative statements and labels. The family found rental accommodation slightly north between La Romaine and San Fernando. One street north of Dumfries Road they found the quaintest little communities. The road started as an unassuming little side road and within a few paces, a sturdily built wooden bridge, then the incline of the road steepened considerably until it plateaued out. The land was relatively flat at the top and the shock was that there were very few structures. Five structures owned by four families, all black families and all the land on the left of the road was owned by the couple's new landlord. This place was so close to the built up network yet it felt like a rural getaway. The open land, fresh air, little animals, fruits. The landlord reared goats and had dogs. This place would be a welcomed change to the family's experiences.

Christmas found the family settled in with all routines learnt and general high spirits all around. The children woke up on Christmas morning to brand new bikes and toys and food fit for the season. They noticed that their parents were relating better and they were glad for the benefits. The small community of age appropriate couples meant that this was the first time the couples would socialize. Thomas loved to put on a show. He lived for these types of occasions. He hated to feel like he was less than others. He would compete to be seen as the best, if he was confident that he could pull it off. He might even show off a little when he got carried away. Most of his actions were harmless except when he started having designs on the other women in the group.

Ruth, being insecure, monitored his movements but liked the new dynamics. No more family and they could finally compare themselves with people who were trying to do the same things as they were. This nostalgic period gave rise to the notion that Thomas wanted to buy a vehicle. The couple discussed it and it was possible due to their combined income. Ruth wanted to help because this was something major that would show that she was an asset to him. She wanted him to be happy. They did not take that long to turn their planning onto a reality. The kids woke up one morning to see their father cleaning his new car. A brown Ford Cortina, locally used but in excellent condition. The only thing that looked better than the car was Thomas strutting around trying to keep it clean.

Ruth hoped that this would settle him down but the opposite became her reality. Though he would not have the car without her, the car was registered and licensed in his name. He could not contain himself as his new car reality went to his head. It soon became 'his' car. He worked shift so transporting his family to school and work was an inconvenience. Soon Ruth realized that she was gaining no benefit from the fact that her husband owned a car. She could not drive and had no license. Soon the car became just another thing that they argued about. The old sentiments had caught up with the new place and now life was hell again.

Ruth distracted herself with the news of a new sibling. She got news from her brother that their sister on their father's side had moved into his area and they were in regular contact. Ruth went to Thomas to ask if he would take the family to meet her sister. He never gave her a straight answer and after a few times she altered her plans. She would travel with the boys. Thomas did not get in her way as he was preoccupied with his own affairs. There they were at the bus station on the San Fernando wharf, Ruth and her four children. After waiting for what seemed like over an hour, the bus came, and people surged forward to the door. The pushing was ridiculous and when Ruth realised that her children were being squeezed, she lost it. She opened her mouth and barked at people and threw her weight around until they stopped briefly and they were all in. Except for risking life and limb, the ride was uneventful from there. The ride to Curepe was long and the children had never travelled this far north before. This was a super adventure for the children. They came off the bus and used another conveyance to their destination, La Horquetta.

La Horquetta was a new National Housing project that featured a specific approach to constructing concrete homes. The first stages of the development had begun but there were plans for massive expansion. Ruth's sister lived on the main Boulevard and after her house a few paces down the Court began. In the shape of a horse shoe. Ruth's brother lived almost in the middle. Ruth's sister welcomed her with the warmth and love of a child denied its siblings. They looked so much alike that even the children felt like they knew her for a long time. She had already started expanding her house and there was plenty of space. The boys met their cousins, two girls, one older than Ruth's oldest and another aged right in the middle of the four boys ages. They all got acquainted and then walked to Ruth's brother's house. Ruth met her sister-in-law again and her nephew, who was around the age of her youngest. She had planned to spend a few days. While she was, there two other siblings came and brought their children. The boys were surrounded by cousins. The days flew by and Ruth's brother drove she and the children home. The children looked at the lights on the highway as they looked through the back window of their uncle's car. Ruth could not help feeling sad to enter her apartment. She had a great visit but her husband would have nothing to do with it.

The general mood of the apartment was tense whether Thomas was home or not. Naturally, things could always get worse. It was unclear if she was looking for something, but she found a pouch full of letters dating back to prior to her marriage to Thomas. The majority of the letters were written while they were together. She sat and read and cried. Read and cried. She had no idea that he had been receiving letters on his job or that he was still in contact with this woman or that their feelings were so strong. She felt sick. How could she compete with this? He wrote to this woman about her too and her children. Rage replaced helplessness but she did not destroy the letters. She put them back just as she had found them. She knew that their marriage was nowhere close to being perfect but now she felt like it was all a lie. The pain was unbearable and she endured it by herself. Who could she tell? Who would listen?

The only remedy for her pain was her routine with the children. Thomas came home less frequently, worked longer hours and had a full slate of social events with family and friends. Ruth drowned in the hopelessness of it all while her husband did not even notice.

CHAPTER TWELVE

SURRENDER

The weight of her thoughts showed on Ruth, and her friends would comment about how aged she looked. Her brain was the new enemy, going around and around with the same thoughts. Never yielding. Never feeling like she had the answer. The obvious was just not practiced. How could she leave him? What would life look like? Then there were his violent reactions but her will to fight was broken. Why fight when all was already lost? Without noticing, she started throwing herself into activities on the job. Union meetings, sports planning and other extracurricular activities. The result being that she was not home early and he was also not home. The children had to tend to themselves.

Her spiral took her to a Guidance Counsellor at the school where she worked. Ruth cried and she spoke, cried and she spoke. Eventually, the counsellor gave her some advice. The counsellor explained that sometimes a woman had to make that break for herself and then come back for the children. Ruth sat and stared.......leave her boys? She did not know if she could do that. She left the counsellor heavier than ever.

It was not long until the clash came. As fate would have it, they were at home while the children went to school. Thomas saw it fit to berate her for her new routine of activities and went so far as to accuse her of being with a "Union man". She saw the opportunity and brought up the letters. Then there it was, no party taking the high road. They shouted, cursed and said every hurtful thing that could be said until he punched her in the face. Her usual reaction would have been to rush him but instead, she ran outside, trying to avoid him. He caught up.

This time was different. Normally she would have rushed him creating a close quarters affair, but now he looked around for an object. He spotted his weapon of choice, a long bamboo and as he clutched it in his hands, he felt powerful. The only thing left was to swing it and he did, across a defending arm and her back and when she fell, her thigh and then he struck her in her head. He heard the sound it made, awareness of his surroundings came back. He had an audience, shocked faces looked on in horror as they were finally introduced to the real man. The image he had built now replaced by a scene of savagery. He dropped the rod and he retreated indoors. She picked herself up and sat on the stairs and cried. The tears flowed for the last time as she vowed to end it. She would no longer be his victim and this was her last helpless cry. Though the scene was charged with emotion for all who witnessed it, no one came over to say or to do anything.

Ruth got up and went inside after he had passed her on the step without a word. He was gone and would not be back soon, free to do as he pleased, as was his custom in times like these. Thomas saw marriage as a prison and at times like this he claimed his independence. She did not care though, it was over and he just did not know it yet. She looked at her options and where there had been trepidation before, now there was only calculation. It took her the greater part of two weeks to prepare and on a day when Thomas was off to work and the kids off to school she stood in the apartment and looked around for the last time. Having taken all her personal documents and some of the children's, his precious letters and other small items, she only had a handbag. Few people could know that she was leaving or they might try to talk her out of it. She confided in two persons that she knew would keep her plan a secret and she was off. Making it to the gate, her focus was shifted to the long walk to where the road descended. Once at this point, she had to get to the bridge. She was almost to the bridge when she saw a figure walk onto the bridge and she froze.

There he stood on the bridge looking up in her direction, a puzzled look on his face. As he slowly walked towards her, she quickened her pace. The tears streamed down now and she could not speak. There was a knot in her throat as she met him all she could muster was "I will be back for you, I promise". It was her eldest son. He had come home early from school. Instinctively he knew what she was doing and he encouraged her to go. Both crying but knowing that this was the only way to secure a future, he let her go. With every step she took away from him she felt ashamed and the weight of her decision came down on her. What kind of woman leaves her children behind? She dug her heels in and determined not to turn back, she crossed the main road and sat in a taxi. She silently cried and trembled as the driver took her off into the unknown.

Meanwhile her son, proud of his reaction, continued up the hill, looking back ever so often, in no hurry to embrace his new reality. He kicked stones as he approached the house. He had been trained his whole life to help his mother and now that she was gone he reasoned that it was now his responsibility to step up. He knew that his father would be in a mess but his concern was really for his three brothers. He worked out that his grandmother was always close and that was the way through.

He got home that evening to an empty apartment and long after securing his brothers from his grandmother's house, they went to sleep that night. Thomas was not home yet. Thomas arrived to find them in bed and his wife absent. He left again and went to his mother's house to complain about the children being left alone while his wife went out. There he confirmed his fears. She was gone. The eldest son had told his grandmother. The shock, he could not see her doing that, she would not leave the boys. He did not think she had it in her to abandon them and now what. He had to take a seat. He would tell everyone that she was the worst mother and that she left four children to take man. She would never see those boys again. He would make her pay for this act of selfishness.

He left that night not knowing what he would do. The next morning, he woke before the children and left. He tried to meet his wife on her way to work to force her to come back home. That morning the children got up, dressed for school and went to their grandmother's house for breakfast and she gave them money to travel to school. Many of the mornings that followed went that way as he tried morning and evening for weeks to catch up with their mother. Eventually he did. Now what could he say to her? He saw the determination in her eyes, he knew that she was not staying in the area, he checked all the possible options. He looked at her and he could not shake the idea that he was so bad that she had to go so far to get away from him. Though she feared him she knew that they were in public and he did not want a scene. While she waited for her bus, he spoke his peace pleading with her for the children's sake to come home, claiming he would be different and that things would work out.

Her response was always measured as she told him that she was never coming back to him. She reminded him of all the times when he left and came back but now it was her turn and she would never turn back. These awkward visits played out several times until Thomas was blindsided by another development. There was a decision on his job that he be moved to another school. The problem was twofold. Firstly, he had worked at his current location for so many years and secondly, the new location was in a closed community in an area in which he knew that he would be in danger. While contemplating the move he went to his mother and brother to get advice and in their deliberations his brother could share some experiences in that rough area. In the end, his brother told Thomas that his life was at risk. Thomas could delay the move for only one week and it was not worth the risk, he had to resign. After working for eight years at that school it was now over. Thomas was spiralling as he never stepped up to be a better parent to children and now he had no job. He neglected to track the bills and his lights were cut by the electricity company, forcing him to sublet electricity from a neighbour downstairs.

Two Christmases after the best Christmas of their lives, the children now endured the worst holiday season of their lives. It had fully sunk in by now that they had no mother and the weight of that was enough without having to cope with their father's denial and absence. The observance of Christmas was at grandma's house which did not feel like home even though they had been spending a lot of time there. The adults ensured that there was enough food and snacks and drinks but the sombre mood hung over the events. Every time an adult reinforced that everything would be all right was a constant reminder that things had crashed and burned and that they were living in the ashes. Thomas had it hardest of all because he was not in a popular position as he exercised his new custodial role by stopping his wife's family from having contact with the children. His actions were now driven by spite and vengeance not caring how his sons felt. The constant now being that only Thomas' feelings mattered.

Things were hardest on his eldest son who thought he could make the sacrifice but he missed his mother most of all. Without her he got no relief, always on duty taking care of three children. He was withdrawn, play seemed to lose its appeal and all the mind did was replay the same sceneries.

He even got into a fight with the neighbour's grandson, on Christmas day of all days. This new arrangement was not working out and it was just a matter of time before it all came crumbling down. Thomas' absence also spoke volumes as he could not console his children and he could barely look them in the eye. His relationship before the separation surely did not help and after he seemed out of his depth. He would not let them see him grieve for a woman that he never really committed himself to love, because he always saw himself as the victim of circumstance. Now he wanted her back. H ow twisted was it that he would give anything for things to return to the way they were. He could not let them see the conflict that was eating out his insides.

CHAPTER THIRTEEN

The Return

One Saturday morning early in January it happened. There was a knock on the the door and there she was. The shock caused the children to pause as they did not know if to open the door or to call their father. She told them to open the door and as they did he came out from the bedroom. She was accompanied by two relatives, her brother and her uncle. The tension was experienced by all parties and the children were afraid. Their father had made statements, violent statements of things he would do if anyone tried to take his children. Ruth spoke to break the awkward silence and begged Thomas to let her take the children. She knew his situation and she knew how hard it must have been for him over the past weeks. She reminded him that he had no plan for their future.

Thomas countered that her plan was no more secure than any that he would come up with and that she was not taking his children. One of the guests suggested that the adult conversation be conducted away from the children and the children were asked to wait outside. After some time the adults brought the children into the house and a decision would be made by including the children's wishes. The children thought it was a bad idea, so the adults must have been truly desperate or blind to the realities of such an arrangement. That day gave rise to the newest power player in the family, Ruth's eldest son. He had studied the choice before him and came up with a plan of his own. He begged his mother not to ask him to answer first but she dismissed his request. What he did not know was that he was critical to the success of her plan. The child's plan was simple, he would sacrifice himself so that his brothers could go with their mother. So when they asked him, he said he would stay. Her eyes bulged, she could not believe what she was hearing. He felt sick. He felt like he had betrayed her and though he was waiting for this day since she left, he had sealed his fate and she would not be a part of his life any more.

The circus continued as they asked the second and he said he would stay with the first. They asked the third and he said that he would stay with the first. The only sane child, the youngest who remembered that this was a no-brainer, at four years old said he wanted to live with his mother. Baring all the talk after this basically decided their fate. The ridiculous decision that Ruth would relinquish custody of a child to Thomas who they both knew was not his, to keep a secret that neither of them were willing to expose at that time. Ruth left with only one of her children, her promise to return fulfilled but feeling hurt and betrayed. She had underestimated Thomas's ability to hate and seek revenge. He did not react with violence but he poisoned her children's minds against her and now he would be raising them.

Victory! What had he won? To this victor there were no spoils, only responsibility. He still had to provide for three children with no salary and no prospects. The posturing now gone, he saw the situation for what it was. Holding on to the boys was yet another way of controlling his ex-wife. She would never be free once he had her children. He was also troubled by his eldest son's decision to stay. That moment created mistrust as Thomas knew to himself his son would not willingly choose him. The deed was done and there was no end game in sight. The only move he had left was one that would diminish him in the worst way, but it was the only play. He had to turn to his mother for help.

Thomas did not know that a conversation was already brewing between two strong power brokers about the fate of his children. Beryl told her mother that she had news. She informed her mother that they were moving. Highly incensed, Ma asked her what would happen to the children up the hill. Beryl, wanting to keep her cards close to her chest, she avoided answering the question. Ma noticed that she got no answer to her question and made her position clear. She stated that she would not be going anywhere without the children. Beryl admired her mother's clarity and conviction at ninety years old. She realised that she had to tell Ma everything. Beryl disclosed that she had found a place big enough for everyone to move into, she just had not told Thomas and Jeremy yet. Ma was relieved as she had been sitting in her dark corner, her eyesight all but gone, but her hearing as sharp as ever. Her experience told her how this had to go and she was proud that her daughter worked things out the same way. Two matriarchs now controlled the show. The chaos would be tamed by old reason. The boys would have to yield to this energy, all five of them, because now this intervention could provide the only sane solution.

Thomas came and laid out his situation and it was important that he ask for help and then they put him at his ease and let him know the plan. Jeremy was not pleased with the idea of sharing a roof with Thomas again, but he understood and agreed. The brothers' issue would have to be buried for the sake of the greater good. All adults were onboard and it did not take them long to mobilise. Thomas did not see his eldest son as a key player in the whole process so on the day of the move the children were in the dark. Beryl had told Thomas to get them ready but following instructions was not his style. Despite many issues on the day, the move was made and the oldest members of the family came through like true heroes.

Vistabella, a small irregularly shaped area between San Fernando and Marabella, provided a strange mix of experiences. It was mostly residential and was hilly but on one side the affluent and the wealthy lived and on the other the grass roots type settled. The family settled at the base of a hill where the rich displayed their affluence. The street had character to it, you could tell that at some time in the past it was upscale and residential. Time changes neighbourhoods though and now the possibility of rentals meant a strange mix of everything, from races, job types and family sizes. The house itself was a three-story house, built to compensate for the extreme slope of the land. The first level was just tall pillars to support the house and two floors above with apartments. The first level just had wash tubs made of concrete and lines to hang clothes after washing. It was also very breezy and shaded. The children spent a lot of time down there playing.

The top floor of the building was left unoccupied and sometimes the landlord would come and spend a few hours there. The family settled in the downstairs apartment or middle level. There were three bedrooms, a large living room area, kitchen, toilet and bath. Beryl had done well. It was almost big enough for four adults and three children. The family made the best of the new arrangement. The real management came from another source. Beryl and Ma had ignored the negative reactions of Beryl's other siblings when they heard of the plan. Now that the move was made the negativity did not stop. Thomas felt completely helpless as these people were his family but they wished that he and his children would just go away and not be around their mother when they came to visit. He tried to be gracious as they gave with one hand and took with another.

Pride always was an integral part of Thomas' psyche. This period felt like hell. He started to spiral even further into self-pity and self-doubt. Silently this help that his mother had given to him was killing him. He was grateful but also ashamed and as far as he could calculate, there was no version of this arrangement that left him feeling whole. The brave face that he put on for the children was not enough to cope with the years of issues shelved between his brother, mother and himself.

CHAPTER FOURTEEN

New Life

The move solved more problems than it created. The overheads were mainly rent and food. The children were now closer to school and walking now became a possibility, which cut out the bill associated with their commute. They thought nothing of it as they embraced their new reality. Thomas was grateful for the resilience of the boys as they stepped up and owned their independence in certain areas. They made friends quickly in the area as school acquaintances noticed their arrival in the neighbourhood. They could walk home with friends, have friends visit them on weekends and visit friends' homes on weekends. This was all new for the boys as their lives were not very social when their mother was around.

Now they were supervised but had more time to pursue their agendas. After all, the adults were overcompensating for the loss of their mother. The boys were kept in check though because Ruth's enforcer was still there. He decided how far the fun would go and when to say enough.

Thomas used this time to teach the boys about caring for fish, tropical fish that he bought in a pet shop. Guppies at first, then mollies, angel fish and fighters. He had a cousin that he would take his eldest son to visit to see how big and healthy these fish could become. He also took the boys on walks to the top of the San Fernando hill, which was close to where they lived. He tried to use this time to connect with the boys but as he tried, he would realise how much ground he had to cover. Though they enjoyed it, the interaction seemed alien, forced somehow because there was no prior context to ground it. Thomas knew he was in a difficult position and he really tried to influence how the boys processed all of this but the more he tried, the more his frustration grew. It all seemed to be bigger than him and coping took everything he had. He decided that he would focus on the eldest who was close to his school placement examination. Months after the move in March they sent him off one morning to write the exam knowing that the events of the past few months and the present could mean disaster for his performance and results. The family was nowhere close to being able to provide a stable environment as a background for this event. Ruth had not abandoned them though as she continued to pay for the lessons that the child had started after school. The teacher was flexible with his payments and she would pay when she could, but her son was tutored like any other student.

Six weeks after the exam, when the results were out, there was an insect problem at the school. The school was closed that Friday and the family did not know that the results were circulated. The newspapers were sold out on that day and they would have to wait until Monday when he went to school to know how he had done. That Friday night at approximately eight thirty Beryl's brother-in-law came running down the stairs and knocked on the door. Jeremy answered and his uncle said that the boy had passed for Naparima College, he saw it in the newspaper, and he run back up the stairs because he left his engine idling. Then he drove off. The silence in the house was interrupted by shouts and screams of joy and laughter. I t was incredible how this could happen. Finally Thomas caught a break, his decision to keep the boys in south Trinidad seemed to be paying off. That night everyone celebrated and took the news as a good thing and they left the implications of the announcement for another day. They deserved this win, they took it without reservation.

The boys continued to settle in nicely, soon they were facilitated with transport to and from school by a family in the area. Everyone became acquainted as Thomas knew the parents and Beryl knew the visiting children and the social network thrived. Beryl particularly liked the part where the children and their parents encouraged her grandchildren to attend church every Sunday. Thomas got busy with the book list for the eldest and he explored the idea of getting used texts books from past students. His cousin helped as he was attending St. Benedict's College at the time and knew students attending Naparima College. Thomas swallowed his pride and went to his family for support to get his son ready for the new school term in September. They all helped as the irony of one of those boys making the family proud was an unexpected twist. They also felt bad to face Beryl and Ma, so this was easier.

Months had passed since the move to Vistabella and though the boys tried to settle in the adults had an unsettled feel about them. Thomas had these irrational mood swings. The pressure prompted him one day to pack up the things belonging to the third boy and he sent him with a message to their mother on her job. He was sending the boy to live with his mother. The eldest boy felt conflicted about this as he could not explain why to his little brother and there was no way for him to not carry out the instructions of his father. When he arrived on his mother's job with his brother and bags, she got angry. She marched them right back stating that was not the arrangement and that she would not put up with Thomas' nonsense. Confused and heartbroken the eldest child did as he was told while he questioned how his father could treat his brother so cold, but this was the second time his mother had the opportunity to take his little brother but left him to live with someone that did not want him. This was another confirmation of a secret that the eldest was living with since he was five, when he found out during an argument that his brother was not his father's son. His mother looked at him but could not speak and never spoke of it after. She probably hoped that he would not remember but it's not the kind of thing that one would forget.

Following the incident Ruth made a visit to the new house. She came when the children were at school and she came to see Beryl, not Thomas. That day they struck a deal for the children to be raised there and Ruth pledged to support them as best as she could. Their agreement was kept between them as Beryl thought she was doing something noble and she knew she needed help that her son could not provide. When Thomas heard that she had visited he was upset and that information weakened the relationship that he had with his mother. Thomas observed as Beryl made more and more decisions about his children while binding him to her decisions.

Thomas' decisions were not all sound and he paid the price for one of them. His anger prompted him to stop all Ruth's family from visiting the children. People they had grown up with, people who could comfort them through their loss, no contact. The eldest was hit hard by the news of his aunt's passing and the anger in him built against his father for denying her access. The confusion surrounding her death was hard to bare because no one would speak to children about such matters. She was gone and everyone was in pain. Loved by everyone in the family, the smallest of women wielding the biggest presence. Nothing about this made any sense since she was active, in her early thirties and the mother of one girl child that meant the world to her. In the middle of all the noise of every selfish life that gathered to mourn her, this was a crippling blow. Though she had one child she left two to mourn as her little brother depended on her for everything. She raised him and now to have to explain to these two children that her absence was permanent seemed unbearable.

Ruth's eldest child stood in the Anglican church yard in his Naparima College uniform as he watched family walk in. He was early for the service, he had not seen these people in a long time. His mother was the one he was waiting to see as this event would bring them face to face again. The day was a sad day but he needed to connect with his mother's family. He resented his father for letting things get this bad. Ruth had just found a sister and now she was burying her big sister, her support and her mother's enforcer. Gone too soon was everyone's sentiment.

Everyone managed as best as they could and the year drew to a close. Ruth had visited the children twice each time bringing groceries and money for their upkeep. It was no surprise that at the end of the year she requested that the children be allowed to spend the Christmas holidays with her. Thomas said nothing and Beryl voiced the opinion that she could do with the break. Once again plans were finalised without Thomas' direct input. He watched as the living arrangement morphed into something that he would not have entertained. He reasoned that because he had no pay check, he had no voice. The school term ended and the children left with their mother. This signalled the final blow to Thomas' ego and he resolved that one way or another going forward, things would be different.

The boys journeyed with their mother in silence, it had been over a year since they spent extended time with her. They eventually recognised their Aunt's house so they knew that they were in La Horquetta and as they passed they were sure that they were going to their uncle's house. They stopped on the horseshoe in between and to their surprise their mother took out keys and opened the door to a house on the street. The boys were pleasantly surprised. It was a two-bedroom apartment with a single bath with a standard sized living room and kitchen. Adequately furnished with the warn feelings of home. The boys felt strange though as they all filed into what was obviously their little brother's room. For the first time the eldest knew what it felt like to be jealous of one of his siblings. They would have to walk across to their uncle's house to be reunited with their little brother.

The reunion meant more to the older boys than the youngest as he was more interested in his normal routine with his cousin, than greeting his brothers. He was now four and had changed so much since they last saw him. The awkward reunion would have to do as he would not sit still to afford anything else. The only thing left was to bring the very long day to a close, so they all returned to their mother's home and sorted sleeping arrangements for the night. The last thing being the list of instructions that their mother gave the eldest as she had to go to work the next morning.

CHAPTER FIFTEEN

Broken

The children woke the next morning to find that their mother had already left for work. The eldest felt conflicted because even though this was all so new it felt more like home that anything in the last year. He knew it was only temporary. The house was stocked with groceries. Their mother had made cakes, Christmas fruit cake and sponge cake. There was ample options of things to drink. The whole scene was surreal because where they had come from, this feeling of belonging had eluded them. The children spared no opportunity to be children as there were too many options to have fun and they could split up. Three houses to visit, cousins with varying interests and adults trying to ensure that they had a great vacation. The eldest did his part, kept the house clean and tracked his brothers movements as best as he could so that when his mother came home in the evening there were good reports. The previous Christmas was horrible but this one proved to be great. The emotional roller coaster continued.

The return to the southland was not easy for the boys but they knew the reality of things. Their mother brought them back well stocked for school. She baked bread and bought all that they would need for the weeks to come. The goodbyes were particularly difficult but they got through that and then life commenced. Slower pace, a lot less joy but commenced. The return to school helped to solidify time tables and routines. The eldest noticed that Thomas was different when they returned but it was not his job to mediate such things, but he noted it. Weeks into the term an unexpected development occurred. Ruth had sent word that she wanted the eldest to come to her job. When he got there his mother explained that she had discussed things with Beryl and Thomas and that his little brother would be coming to live with them in south Trinidad. The eldest could not understand and when he asked he was just told to do as she said. This helped him to cope with her previous decision to send back his other brother. He reasoned that she really wanted her children to grow together. When he got home there were no answers as the adults betrayed nothing, and now there were four of them again.

Months later brought clarity, the company that Thomas had previously worked for and that Ruth was currently working for would undergo massive downsizing offering 'separation packages' to a lot of workers. Ruth would soon be out of a job. To her credit she acted early and put things in place for her survival. She gave up the house and moved into her sister's house and she had already made the adjustment for her son to be in south with the other boys. She was luckier than most though as she was able to get employment at her credit union to help with some special projects. This allowed her to be around in south and the eldest took advantage of this and visited her regularly as it was walking distance from his school. This was a trying time for Ruth and she put on a brave face, but it was taking a toll on her.

The eldest had spent so much time focusing on what was happening with his mother that he completely neglected to observe what was going on with Thomas. Things continued to spiral out of Thomas's control, and he resented that fact and the people responsible. He felt sick to own the fact that he resented his own children for not seeing the effort that he was making and their blind loyalty to their mother was a problem for him. He was a broken man with no job prospects, no money, no plan and he saw himself as a burden on the arrangement at home there. The eldest had noticed that he would not be home every night and that there were missing periods that went unaccounted for. It all came to a head one day when the eldest came home from school to an argument between his father and grandmother. The result was that Thomas started packing the few belongings that he had and appeared to be leaving.

His son asked him what was going on and as his father looked at him he could see the conflict in his eyes. He could see that his father blamed him for not being loyal to him but there were no tears, just the resolve to say his piece. Thomas told his son that it was time for him to go, as he could not turn his luck around and he could not contribute. The least he could do was reduce the amount of mouths to feed. He said that he had met someone who would help him get back on his feet and that this was best for everyone. Within that moment the eldest knew that he did not want his father to go. He had an emotional spike of fear and rage which quickly subsided because of the broken man that stood before him. Both hearts breaking because they could not get what they wanted. In the end the eldest stood there and looked on as his father put his bag on his back and walked up the stairs. This was the second time that he stood and watched a parent walk away from him. He could not be supportive or proud this time because he felt so alone. He felt abandoned and without hope.

How could he do anything but give up hope? What had started with uncertainty some thirteen years prior with a young man and woman now lay in ruins, leaving four lives destined for even more uncertainty. The only safety net being two old matriarchs, members of the old guard, strong and resolute in their resolve to persevere. They would steady the ship, make the deals and keep on keeping on. After all, they lived for the wins and were battle hardened enough to weather any storm................

CHAPTER SIXTEEN

Focus

Thomas approached the apartment in Cocoyea with a heavy heart. He knew that this was based on running away from a situation rather than running towards this. He knew that he was going to commit himself in a way that he could never get out or repay. Necessity dictated that he should do this and he tried to convince himself that he would be of more value here than where he left. The lure was a woman from his past that he had been intimate with. She had now fallen on some difficult times socially where the father of her two girl children was absent and she needed a man in the house to fill the void. The two-bedroom apartment was small and privacy was an issue as access to the kitchen or living room lead through the two bed rooms. The necessary acclimatisation period had passed and all parties knew the plan. The elder girl was least pleased and showed her displeasure. The younger girl was different, eager to please both her mother and anyone sanctioned by the mother. Without knowing it she was the mother's greatest asset in trying to secure her agenda. The three of them would make it a home while ignoring the detractor.

Thomas' woman was a pre-school teacher who had become the administrator of the school. She took care of the bills from this income and was very frugal with money, some might even say, cheap. These settings caused Thomas to dig deep. He knew what he left behind and knew he still had to contribute somehow and now, he had to help where he was living. He went to his mentor, an older man, more versed in matters of marriage and divorce and reconstituted families and he sought guidance. The man took him to the back of his house and showed him some empty pieces of land overrun with bush. Thomas understood that he had to do things differently. The land was "state land" and Thomas was no thief but he would clear a section, about half a lot and start planting food to feed his family.

From that point, things progressed quickly. Within a few weeks he cleared a portion of land and started planting peas, corn, cassava, ochroes, tomatoes and he ensured that he adhered to the times in his almanac calendar. He was actually very good at this new pursuit and worked very hard to make it a reality. He had not gotten any crops yet from his new garden but he was proud of what he was able to accomplish. While this was being developed, he realised that he had not visited his mother in a while and it was important to introduce his new partner. When they arrived there was no surprise as Beryl recognised the woman. No longer that young Indian girl from La Romaine, and she knew that she had to be careful with this individual. Beryl's concern was for the well being of her grandchildren. She could not be the normal accommodating person that she usually was.

The introductions were made and the actors assessed their roles as this was the beginning of a long and drawn-out affair. The children were supposedly at the centre of this charade but were oblivious to most of the agendas of the adults, least of all Beryl who paid the price of being mediator between Thomas and his separated spouse. The economic needs of the day coloured many decisions and 's loyalty and integrity were often called into question. Her only saving grace was that she made a decision and resolved to survive after doing so.

Thomas and his social juxtaposing took place while the national landscape was turbulent at best. Things came to a head on July 27th, 1990 when the NAR (National Alliance For Reconstruction) government was attacked by the Jamaat Al Muslimeen. The attempted Coup lasted six days but the resulting curfew lasted for months. This period was significant to the family because in September, Ma got sick. She had contracted the flu. Everyone in the house had the flu actually and she had to deal with the virus at ninety-three (93). Her children could only visit when the curfew had lifted every day. She struggled for about two weeks and eventually got pneumonia. The family had talks about moving her to a nursing home but Ma did not want that, she wanted to be home. On the 20th September at approximately eleven pm Beryl went into the room to check on her mother and found that she was lying still barely breathing. Beryl spoke to her softly and told her that she had deceived her, she begged her not to leave. As she held Ma's hand she heard her take her final deep breath and then nothing. Ma was gone. She took a few moments with her mother and then quietly she told Jeremy and the eldest boy as they were still awake. The three of them filed into the room and said their final goodbyes. They could not move the body until six in the morning. This was the oldest member of their family. The calmest and strongest under fire from life's assaults. Who would they be without her? Who would Beryl be without her? Sun rise would answer both questions.

The news gave rise to chaos as grief meant malicious name calling and finger pointing to Beryl's siblings and family. This shielded their own guilt for not doing more for their mother by attacking the person who had done the most. This was their way and the ritual had to play out. Despite the fact that they had celebrated a life of calm, dignified behaviour by acting in the most chaotic, vengeful manner, they found that their behaviour was justified and possibly overdue. The eye of the storm was always where Cathleen could be found, seemingly innocent while feeding the winds to ferocious speeds and certain destruction. They would have their final revenge for taking in those bastard children.

The funeral passed without incident and everyone assembled at the cemetery with a cold finality. Everyone assembled at Beryl's sister's house while never betraying this to Beryl's family. The aftermath of the funeral was working out exactly how they did it. The last moment of their mother's memorial was stolen from Beryl. Her children's names notably left out of the funeral program and an empty house where the people who lived with Ma mourned silently, both for the loss of the Matriarch and for the end of the family.

Thomas lost himself in his garden. It was the only thing that brought positive results. He worked hard and in the short term the only thing he could show for it was weight loss. He was never obese so this made him look sick. He would avoid as many people as possible. His pride never really left. The fact that he came home to a woman every day, who expected something while never asking made living there very stressful. Yet, he was committed to proving everyone wrong. He felt a weight lifted off his shoulders the first day he could bring produce home with him. Peas, a short crop, was abundant on his little piece of land. Bags and bags of peas, he felt like he had done it. Finally, around the corner, the worst was over. Then other crops came in. Before long he was cultivating approximately twenty-three items on that small parcel of land.

His trips to his mother's residence were infrequent after Ma's passing but now he was eager to visit. He brought food and his children were both glad to see him and grateful for his contribution. He even took the eldest son onto the land and showed him what he had been up to. The boy had mixed feelings as he was proud that his father was so good at planting but he still felt like his father had abandoned him. He did not know where he lived and was not a part of his life really. The token trip to the garden and vegetables were a poor substitute for a father. He kept it mostly to himself and gave his father what he realised he was craving, encouragement and validation. These were like gold to Thomas to counter

97

his self-doubt and hopelessness. His son did notice how much this meant to him and he could not take that away.

This act was never ending. The constant need to do the mature thing, the right thing in every situation. The eldest boy tried to live up to some kind of standard but one person who resented him for his pretense was his little brother. They were just two years apart and he saw through the nonsense. He often challenged why everyone deferred to the eldest and why he always had to listen to his every command. He started to push back. When Thomas was not around he refused to accept his big brother as some kind of substitute guardian. They started to have clashes. Life was cruel to the younger brother though because although they were just two years apart his big brother was a growth spurt ahead of him. Inevitably their conflict led to the eldest being physical with the younger stubborn sibling. It never went on for too long because Beryl was always there to break it up as it started. There seemed to be no justice though because the eldest was Beryl's enforcer as well. Thomas was called in after a few of these incidents.

When he arrived he did not know what he was going to say. Everything was a mess and he wore that on his sleeve. He started to address the issue, then the form of the events slipped away from him. He tried to speak to both children like equals, first mistake. He tried to tell them that, as brothers, they should never be at each other's throats, second mistake. The scene changed by this time because the eldest felt like he was being accused of doing something wrong. He was the enforcer and they had all used him in that capacity. If anyone was tearing down the fabric of their reality it was the little brother and he had to be set straight. He was the good soldier and would not be thrown under the bus. For the first time in a long time, he realised that he was defending himself and not the collective of boys. He broke form and Thomas' issues were no longer his concern. He attacked his father with his words. Let him know that he had abandoned them and now was showing up out of the blue to discipline them. He spoke his heart, which for this little boy was never a good thing as his heart was always too heavy with sorrow. He blamed his father for all the decisions that blew up in their faces and for their current plight. When he was done, everyone was spent. Thomas was done. He could dispute none of it and it took a special type of human being to turn that moment into a teachable moment. He knew how his son felt now, that was the only takeaway. In the end he questioned why he even came.

A week had passed, and everyone was trying to forget what had happened. The boys stopped fighting as the younger boy realised that he could not break the system, so he conformed. The eldest was still angry all the time but felt bad that he had treated his father that way. He wondered if he would ever come back and blamed himself for pushing him away. The general mood was uncertain and then they received a visitor. Thomas's new partner had come to visit. This upset everyone because she came alone. This was new, she was not welcome there like that. She spent some time talking to Beryl first and then they called the eldest boy to join their conversation. She reported that she was worried about Thomas. Since he left, he had not been eating or sleeping well and he was acting as though he could have a mental breakdown. His son loved his father but did not trust this woman. He knew that the things he said to his father were dangerous and devastating but he did not like this woman. Why should he help her sort out her household. He could not abandon his father. In the end he went with her.

He found Thomas in bed, weak and frail and almost unresponsive. He sat next to him and he said that he was sorry. He said that he should not have said those things and that he needed him in his life. He told him that the garden was suffering and that he would help him. Within the hour he had dressed and they left for the garden and they never spoke of those events ever again.

CHAPTER SEVENTEEN

Priorities

Things needed to change if new family arrangement were to work out in Cocoyea. The first was a change of apartment, to a location not very far from where they were. The difference was that Thomas did not have to walk through the girls' bedroom anymore to get to the living room. The girls still had the option to walk through their mother's room but did not have to, as there was an alternative route to the kitchen and living room. Thomas still was not providing an income so there was no opportunity to plan better as there was no room for guests. His partner made herself comfortable as all this was still a product of her family plan and a nuclear approach.

Thomas went along as he remembered that she was paying for everything and he was fortunate to be included.

The garden was thriving and Thomas could feel great about his role now as they even started planting things in the yard where Beryl lived. There was peas and corn and cassava in the back yard. There was no significant increase in money but there was lots to eat. If things had improved at Beryl's house then they were surely better where Thomas was staying. The monkey was not completely off Thomas' back though. He knew he had not worked in what seemed to be approaching three years. When he least expected it, his mentor came through with some news. The local telephone company had inhouse security and were hiring. This was a good opportunity since they paid better than private firms and there were benefits. He took his shot. He kept it close to his chest though and after interviewing and training, he was hired on probation. He was back. Months after their move to the new house and he was working again.

He finally told Beryl and the boys and they were happy for him. This was great news, but it had little bearing on the children's plight as his new income benefitted where he lived. It was not long until his partner complained that attendance at the pre-school was falling and she could not manage the bills any more. She soon closed the school to stay at home as a homemaker to take care of Thomas and her two children. The garden was no more as it was overgrown with bush in a short time. When Thomas visited Beryl's house they usually argued about some aspect of the role that he was neglecting with the children. His partner's advice was that if his mother upset him that much, he did not have to go visit. She secured her future and her children's future at the expense of his children's survival.

Generally Thomas worked with the premise that his progress was divorced from the activities of the children. This was made worse by the news of developments on their mother's side which he usually found out after the fact. He treated the children as though they were secretive, but he could hardly expect different after he would berate and denigrate their mother in front of the people he lived with. He was particularly upset about the children spending time in Laventille when he found out that his ex-wife had a new partner and he was not informed. Strange position to take as Thomas never really put anything in place to reach him. He showed up when he showed up, as though life was on pause when he was absent. These episodes made him bitter and distant. He used them though as they gave him the opportunity to do what he ultimately wanted to do, which was focus on himself.

The new development with Ruth prompted her to visit him on work. He was surprised to see her but he soon realised that she was there to discuss the final dissolution of their marriage. She knew he would never initiate things so she had and she offered to pay for it as well. She just needed him to consent and put things in place for the children financially. He had an issue with both things but the latter rather than the former was the real sticking point. As they reasoned it the children were in a neutral home with Beryl and he just had to agree to a modest sum per week and the matter would be over. Thomas could not let her get what she wanted so easily. He had to drag it out, play games as was his habit. She stayed her course and despite how many visits it took, she was determined to dissolve the marriage.

He thought she had plans to marry again and that gave him leverage. She kept her cool as she knew that he would try to make it impossible but she drew comfort from the fact that this was the last thing. Thomas did notice that she had changed and that she weathered his taunting and stalling with an ability that she never displayed before. His concern was that she would not claim any of his earnings. Everything else was just a little payback. Ruth had been living in Laventille for almost three years when her partner got sick. He died at Port of Spain hospital after being diagnosed with a brain tumour. Without him, her life changed again and she moved back in with her sister.

The prospect of finalizing a divorce seemed to pale in comparison to figuring out the next steps. Ruth had been stumped by the developments and she felt stuck. Ironically, now that Thomas became aware of the developments through his children, he agreed to the divorce. She closed that chapter and pressed on to the next. She felt like there was only one thing that she had not tried. One last move. She would migrate to find work to take care of her children. People would not understand or they may have criticised her for doing it but her mother did it and that is how she was raised. She was finally in that place to give it a try.

Ruth spoke to her eldest about it and briefed him on the plan. He was sad but she was determined. She planned things so that her brother, sister and her son were at the airport to see her off. Her son stood there in the waving gallery of the airport and watched his mother get on the plane. He wondered, how many times would he say goodbye to his parents..........

AUTHOR'S NOTE

The book is done in a retro time line. Therefore the concept of looking back is featured in the name, 'Sankofa'. The fact that Trinidad and Tobago is the most southerly islands in the West Indian Island chain accounts for the story being a 'Southern tale'. That and the fact that it is based in south Trinidad. The retro theme is aided by the retro pictures. Care was taken to respect History even though this is not an account of history but rather fiction set in time pockets.

The story tracks a character in the hope of understanding what each stage of his development adds to his personality. That ever emerging personality makes choices that has consequences. Family is a recurring theme in the story and their role keeps morphing as things develop. The main characters have been given names while supporting characters need not be named as they carry out their roles in the story.

I am grateful that many stories can form one story and for the synergy preserved by this sharing of stories. The author hopes that at some point the reader may be able to identify with one or more of the characters as they serve to provoke thought and ideas about implication and other possible reactions to the decisions made.

The book was born of the ever-present need for us to look at ourselves and the cumulative effect of our decisions. To look at our deeds is the early development on route to owning our part in the painting of life's masterpiece. We are all influencing our environment while being affected by it and this tale serves to capture the nuances of this arrangement.

SANKOFA

If hindsight improves vision.
Unravels the situation,
Minus opinion or speculation.
Findings bound to one conclusion.
Then what of the mission?
When conclusion after conclusion,
We stumble through our action,
Ignoring actual projection.
Could it possibly help our situation,
To go back to first decision?
Revisit original intention
To minimise error in our opinion.
Correcting speculation,
We may gain control of our reaction.
Though we again fall short of a solution,
We may be better able to accept our place
In the current conundrum.

By J.K. Pascall

In Loving Memory
R.I.P.

We trust that you enjoyed: Sankofa, A Southern Tale

For other works by J.K. Pascall
Published by authorHouse:

Try,

Living Through 2016: Beyond Fiction

Or

Dialogue: From Mind's Heart to Yours

CPSIA information can be obtained
at www.ICGtesting.com
Printed in the USA
BVHW031154100419
545159BV00006B/28/P